# ANIMAL RESCUE

## The Pampered Rabbit

# TINA NOLAN

**Stripes**

# ANIMAL MAGIC
## RESCUE CENTRE

## MEET THE ANIMALS IN NEED OF A HOME!

### SALLY AND SARA

What a handsome pair! These two friendly and inquisitive bunnies are looking for new homes.

### COCOA

Dumped beside a rubbish skip and left to starve, Cocoa loves to be groomed. Totally delicious!

### SNOWFLAKE

A lovely roly-poly cat with a soft coat. She loves ball games. Are there any football fans out there?

 SITE SEARCH

 NEWS

 HELP US

 CONTACT

 DONATE!

# BILLY AND BEAUTY

Two fluffy abandoned guinea pigs. Can you give these playmates a home together?

# PARKER

This gorgeous old chap loves to sleep. He's looking for a nice quiet home to retire in.

# LILY

Lily's all alone in the world. Can you give her the loving home she needs?

# Chapter One

"Jump, Holly, jump!" Eva stood in the yard at Animal Magic, training Holly to leap through a hoop.

Holly was the Harrisons' black and white Border collie pup. She raced towards the hoop, then screeched to a halt. She sat and stared at it, her head cocked to one side.

"You didn't jump," Eva said with a disappointed frown. At this rate, Holly's agility training would never take off.

"Try lowering the hoop," Eva's dad, Mark, suggested as he led Peggy the pony out of the stables.

*Clip-clop, clip-clop* – Peggy's hooves sounded hollow. Holly pricked up her ears and ran to investigate.

"Here, Holly! Good dog!" Eva called. On the list for this morning's training routine were the weave poles and see-saw, as well as the hoop.

Agility training was Eva's latest Big Idea.

"Holly's learned how to sit and do all the basics," she'd explained to her mum, dad and brother, Karl, at teatime the day before. "Now I want to train her to do more complicated stuff."

Karl had given one of his big-brother snorts. "Eva found a website on agility training," he explained to his parents. "She was on it for hours. It shows pictures of dogs on see-saws and dogs crawling through tunnels. She reckons Holly is going to be a champion!"

"Isn't she a bit young?" Heidi had asked, glancing at Holly curled up on her bed by the kitchen fire. "Don't dogs have to be fully grown before they can officially enter agility tests?"

But Eva's dad had encouraged her. "You can never start them too young, eh, Eva? Holly might be a puppy prodigy, for all we know!"

So here she was, on a cold Saturday morning in March, her red jacket zipped up to her chin, trying to persuade Holly to jump through a hoop.

"Here, Holly!" she called again. This

time the puppy obeyed. She ran back to
Eva and wagged her tail.

Meanwhile, Mark tied up Peggy and
went inside to muck out her stable.

Eva held the bright green hoop close
to Holly's nose. "Smell this. It's made of
plastic. And all you have to do is jump
right through the middle!"

Holly sniffed and gave the hoop a lick.

"You – through – here!" Eva explained
carefully. Then she spotted Karl coming
out of Reception. "Hey, can you hold
this for me?" she called.

Reluctantly, he came over and took
the hoop from Eva. "Like this!" she told
Holly.

She scrambled clumsily through it,
then turned to face her. "Da-dah!"

*Yip!* Holly said, with an excited wag of

her tail. But she didn't move.

"Brilliant!" Karl laughed. "Just like on the website – not!"

Eva's feelings were hurt. "I don't know why you're laughing," she said. "You should be helping me to train Holly, not making fun."

Karl shrugged. "Like Mum said, she's too little for agility training, aren't you, Holls?" He leaned forward and patted her.

"You're just making excuses not to bother," Eva argued. "You won't be laughing when Holly becomes the youngest champion ever!"

*Yip!* Holly barked, her brown eyes sparkling.

Just then, a car turned into the yard off Okeham Main Street. A man and a girl climbed out.

"Hiya, Karl!" the dark-haired girl called, waving at him.

Eva saw her brother's face turn red.
She recognized the pretty newcomer as
Mia Logan — a girl in the same class
as Karl at Clifford Comprehensive.
"What's she doing here?" she whispered.

"The Logans are moving to Okeham,"
he hissed back. He picked up Holly and
held her close as if he was trying to hide
behind her. "Today, actually!"

"So this is Animal Magic?" the tall
man said as he glanced at the stables,
the cattery, kennels and the porch
leading into the reception area. "I hear
you have a great set-up — Mia's told me
all about it."

"Thanks for promising us the hay for
Fern's new hutch." Mia breezed up to
Karl.

"One less thing for us to think about,"

Mr Logan explained to Eva. "Moving house is hectic enough, without having to remember to stock up with things like hay, so we really appreciate the help."

"Come with me," Karl told Mia, thrusting Holly into Eva's arms and leading Mia towards the stables.

"Mia's mad about her rabbit," Mr Logan continued. "She can hardly bear to be separated from her. Fern gets only the best food and bedding. And we just bought her a brand-new hutch."

Eva smiled and nodded. She watched Karl carry the overflowing bag out of the stable. "Watch out for Peggy!" she warned.

The little chestnut pony suddenly reached out and took a mouthful of hay from Karl as he passed. Mia grabbed

Karl's arm as if she was scared. Karl's
face grew redder still.

"Here, let me," Mr Logan said, striding across the yard to take the bag from Karl. "Come on, Mia, let's get a move on. There are a million and one jobs to do back at the new house."

Quickly, they thanked Karl, put the hay in the boot, then drove off.

"So?" Eva demanded as Mr Logan drove off.

"So – what?" Karl muttered, picking pieces of hay from his sleeve.

"You're blushing red – red – red!" Eva laughed.

Karl frowned, then glared at her. "Am not!" he mumbled as he stalked off. "You stick to dog training, Eva. Concentrate on Holly, why don't you?"

# Chapter Two

"Mark and I have decided to hold a spring party!" Heidi announced later that morning. She stood in Reception with Eva, Karl and their grandad, Jimmy Harrison.

"Cool!" Karl and Eva cried.

"Not next Saturday, but the one after – to celebrate Animal Magic's success," Heidi explained. "And to thank everyone who has helped to make it happen over the last year."

"Great idea. We'll design an invite and put it up on the website." Karl got busy straight away.

"Print some out so we can hand them round the village." Eva couldn't wait — an Animal Magic party would be super-cool!

"Jen will be back by then, so she can help us celebrate, too."

"Where is Jen?" Jimmy asked as Eva sat with Karl to work on the invites.

"She's on a course," Heidi replied. "She wants to update her knowledge on small animal care."

"Eva, how did you get on with Holly this morning?" Mark interrupted as he came in from the yard. "Did she eventually jump through the hoop?"

Holly sat on her bed, ears pricking up

when she heard her name.

"Hah!" Karl grinned. "Do pigs fly?"

Heidi looked out of the window as a vehicle similar to Mark's own delivery van pulled off Main Street. "Mark, isn't that Stephen Jennings? I wonder what he's doing here."

They didn't have long to wait to find out. They saw Mark's workmate jump out of his van, carrying what looked like an injured dog wrapped in a blanket.

Eva ran out with her mum and dad to help. She held the door while Stephen carried the dog into Reception.

"I found her in the car park at the back of the big chocolate factory in Okeham," Stephen explained. "I was delivering parcels when I spotted her lying beside a rubbish skip."

"Good work, thanks for bringing her in," Mark said, watching anxiously as Heidi led the way into an examination room and asked Stephen to place the dog on the table.

Eva gasped when she saw the state the poor dog was in. It was a dark brown cross-breed without a collar, so thin that you could see her ribs, with a big cut across the pad of her front paw. Her eyes were glazed over.

"This looks serious," Heidi said quietly, glancing up at Mark with a worried look in her eye.

"Eva, run to the house and bring my white coat. Check that the stethoscope is in the pocket. Mark, would you fetch the stand for a fluid drip? Stephen, I'm sure Jimmy would take you over to the

house and make you a coffee, if you'd like one…"

For the next hour Eva watched anxiously as her mum worked. Would she be able to revive the poor, starving dog and patch up the gash on her foot? She stayed in the examination room while Heidi attached the drip, then stitched the wound. All the while, the patient lay with her eyes half closed.

"Eva, can you fetch a clean blanket?" Heidi would ask. Or, "Stroke her head and speak to her gently while I clean the cut. That's right."

"You're going to be fine," Eva whispered to the dog. "We'll look after you and make you better."

"Her heartbeat is stronger," Heidi announced after she'd finished the sutures. "I've given her an injection of antibiotics to clear up any infection."

"Will she be OK?" Eva breathed. The dog's eyes were fully open now and she was trying to lift her head. Heidi nodded. "Let's hope so. I can only say one thing for certain — she wouldn't have got through another night if Stephen hadn't brought her in."

"Did I hear my name being mentioned?" Stephen Jennings asked as Karl showed him into the examination room.

"Mum says you're a hero — you saved her life!" Eva exclaimed.

"Did I really?" Stephen beamed. "That's good to hear."

"She's not microchipped, so as soon as she's well enough, we'll put her on our website for someone to adopt," Eva rushed on. "She needs a name. What would you like to call her?"

"Me?" Stephen blushed. He seemed pleased to be asked. "Well, I suppose since I found her at the chocolate factory, and because she's a lovely dark brown colour, we could call her Cocoa."

"Cool," Karl agreed.

Eva grinned. She stroked the patient's soft, floppy ears. "Did you hear your new name, Cocoa? You're going to get well soon, and we're going to find you a perfect new home."

# Chapter Three

As soon as Cocoa seemed to be through the worst, Eva dashed back to the house to find Holly. The puppy was at the door, waiting for her with a sad "Where have you been?" expression.

"I know – I've been ages!" Eva admitted, kneeling down to give her a cuddle. "We had an emergency in the surgery. But I'm here now. And listen, Holly, I've had another idea – I realize it was hard for you to learn to jump through the hoop, so I've decided we should join an agility training club!"

*Yip!* Holly loved being cuddled and stroked. She licked Eva's hands.

"I'm going to look on the Kennel Club website!" Eva declared. "It'll tell us where our nearest club is. There'll be lots of other dogs learning to run through tunnels and do the weave poles. You'll be able to copy them!"

"In the meantime, has Holly had her morning walk?" Mark asked as he came downstairs into the kitchen.

"Oops – no!" Eva realized they'd all been too busy. "I'll take her now."

"Karl's almost ready to print out the party invites and he wants your final approval," her dad reminded her, as Eva grabbed Holly's lead and led her out of the house. "So don't be too long."

"I'll be back before you know it!" Eva called. She strode out of the yard.

"Hi, Eva! Hi, Holly!" Annie Brooks called from next door.

Holly heard Annie's voice and tugged at the lead. Together, she and Eva joined Annie, who was dressed in her favourite Animal Magic sweatshirt and jeans.

"Snap!" Eva grinned, unzipping her jacket.

"Keep the Saturday after next free — we're having an Animal Magic party!" she announced. "Tell your mum and dad. Tell everybody!"

Annie nodded. "OK, I'll mention it to the Logans. I'm going to Earlswood Avenue with Mum in a minute to help them move in. Mum is Mrs Logan's best friend."

"That's nice," Eva said, eager now to be on her way. "See you later!" She waved at Linda Brooks, who had just come out of the house, then at George Stevens, turning in to the yard at Animal Magic on his bike.

"Is Karl in?" George yelled.

Eva nodded. At this rate she'd never

get down to the riverside. "Come on, Holls, let's go!" she said, setting off at a brisk walk.

Half an hour later, Eva was back at home. She had the next part of her day planned out, and first up was checking on the Kennel Club website for a local agility training club.

"Phone call for you," her dad said as she walked through the kitchen door. He held out the phone.

"Hi again, Eva," Annie said. "You have to come up to Earlswood Avenue!"

"Hi, Annie. What's wrong? Has something happened?"

"No, nothing bad. But you totally have to come and see Fern."

"I'm a bit busy. Maybe later." Eva chose a cheese and pickle sandwich from a plate on the table. She took a big bite.

"But Fern is totally gorgeous!" Annie exclaimed. "Eva, Mia's got Fern a big new hutch with a living area and a separate bedroom and feeding platform. Mr Logan is going to build a run in the garden. It'll be really cool!"

"Sounds good," Eva admitted.

"Better than good, Eva!" Annie was bubbling with excitement. "This is a rabbit mansion! And Fern is just so adorable – you've got to come and see!"

It was no good – Eva couldn't resist. Quickly she told Holly to lie in her bed. "Give me ten minutes," she told Annie. "I'll be there!"

Eva rode up to Earlswood Avenue on
her bike, pedalling hard up the hill and
getting off outside the house where a big
removal van was parked. She removed
her helmet, then stood aside as two men
carried a sofa down the ramp.

"Hi, Eva – you'll be so glad you came!"
Annie cried, running down the drive to
meet her. "Mia's helping Fern to get used
to her new hutch – come and see!"

So Eva followed Annie around the side
of the house into the back garden, where
they found Mia kneeling by a big new
two-storey rabbit hutch. In her arms
she held a soft, caramel-coloured rabbit,
with long floppy ears and big dark eyes.

"Now Fern, this is your new home,"

Mia was saying. "You have a downstairs bit, where you can sit and see what's going on in the garden. Then you walk up the ramp here, into your bedroom, where it's nice and cosy."

"Isn't she cute?" Annie whispered to Eva as they joined Mia and Fern. "Look at those lovely floppy ears!"

Eva smiled. She loved Fern's big dark eyes and her soft brown nose, her long whiskers and her drooping ears. "She looks kind of sad," she said softly.

"Fern is a dwarf lop," Mia told them, letting them stroke the rabbit. "She's a year old and she won't grow any bigger. She weighs just over two kilos."

"She's lovely!" Eva sighed. "How long have you had her?"

"Since she was a baby," Mia explained. "She wasn't very well at first – the vet in Okeham said she hadn't been given the right food to eat at the place where we bought her, so since then I've given her the best of everything – the best muesli, the best hay, the best fruit and vegetables…"

"In other words, you spoil her!" Annie laughed.

"That's what Mum and Dad say," Mia confessed with a slow smile. "But I can't help it, can I, Fern?"

"This has to be the best hutch as well!"

Eva grinned as she inspected Fern's new home. "I like the bedroom — it's nice and high off the ground."

Mia nodded. "It keeps her dry and it means foxes can't get near her. I've lined the floor with wood shavings and hay, so she can snuggle up at night."

"Cool!" Annie was impressed.

"I've put her food bowl in the compartment next to the bedroom so she won't have far to go if she wakes up hungry. And her water bottle fixes on to the wire netting. It even fits into a little padded sleeve, so the water won't freeze in winter!"

"I like it!" Eva said. "I wonder if Fern knows how lucky she is."

"Let's see," Mia said quietly, deciding

that it was time to let her rabbit explore her new hutch. She asked Annie to open the door, then she placed Fern inside and closed the door behind her.

At first Fern crouched on the cold grass and twitched her nose.

Eva noticed she was shivering. "The poor little thing's not sure what's going on," she murmured. "Everything is so new."

"It's OK, Fern," Mia whispered. "It's safe to take a look around."

The small rabbit blinked, then took one hop forward. She sniffed at the ground, then at the wooden ramp leading to the upper level.

"I put some chopped apple and carrots in her food bowl," Mia whispered to Eva and Annie. "I'm hoping the smell will attract her."

Sure enough, Fern placed her front paws on the ramp and sniffed the air.

"Yummy carrots!" Annie breathed.

Eva willed Fern to carry on.

Hop-hop – she was halfway up the ramp.

She twitched her nose, smelling the hay in the bedroom. Hop-hop – up the ramp and out of sight.

"Yesss!" Mia, Annie and Eva grinned happily.

They heard Fern rustle through the sawdust and hay, and waited for her to follow her nose, out through the bedroom door on to the feeding platform. Sure enough, a small brown nose and a pair of long whiskers soon appeared.

"Sooo sweet!" Annie whispered.

Though it was cold and windy in Mia's garden on the hill, Eva felt a warm glow inside her. She watched Fern emerge from her sleeping quarters, her brown eyes shining, her lovely caramel coat gleaming in the sunlight.

As soon as Fern spotted the dish of fruit and veg, she made a dash across the platform. Hop-hop, hop-hop. She was there and tucking in, head down, with her sharp teeth chomping.

"Cute!" Eva beamed. "Thanks for inviting me, Annie. I wouldn't have missed this moving-in day for anything!"

# Chapter Four

"Fern's fur is pale brown — like toffee ice cream!" Eva gushed. "She's got big, big brown eyes and the cutest nose…!"

"Yeah, yeah — don't go on about it," Karl told Eva as they sat in Reception next morning. "I saw the rabbit myself, if you must know."

Eva looked surprised. Then she felt silly for showering Karl with every detail of Fern's appearance. "Really? How come?"

"I was at George's house yesterday. He lives next door, remember."

"But that doesn't explain how you actually saw Fern. She didn't escape into George's garden, did she?" Eva knew that George Stephens had a rabbit of his own who might not be too friendly towards a newcomer.

"No, don't stress," Karl insisted. He was busy entering some new arrivals on the Animal Magic website. "Billie and Beauty – two fluffy abandoned guinea pigs…"

"So?" As usual, once Eva had her teeth into a subject, she didn't let go.

"So, George and me – we happened to look over the fence while Mia's dad was building the rabbit run." Karl concentrated on the keyboard. "Can you

give these playmates a home together?"
he typed.

"Oh, you just happened to look!" Eva
exclaimed. "Don't tell me – I expect you
offered to lend Mr Logan a hammer and
some nails. Next thing you knew, you
just happened to be having a cosy chat
with Mia again!"

"Actually no," Karl muttered.

Eva wasn't really being mean when
she teased Karl about Mia – in fact
she'd quite like him to have a girlfriend,
she decided. And Mia Logan seemed
nice, with her shiny, dark cropped hair
and warm smile. "Anyway, what did
you think of Fern?" Eva rubbed the top
of the counter with an antiseptic wipe,
ready for the next arrival. So far this
morning, they'd taken in Billie and

Beauty, plus a black dog called Parker and a white cat called Snowflake. Poor Parker had been left behind when his elderly owner had moved into a care home, while Snowflake had come to them from an empty house in Clifton.

"Fern's sweet," Karl said. He logged off and stood up, setting off for the intensive care unit where they were still keeping an eye on Cocoa's progress. "But I wouldn't go over the top the way you, Annie and Mia do," he added as he left.

"Hi, Mum – how's Cocoa?" Eva called later that morning. She was in the yard with Holly, still teaching her the hoop trick. Holly had made friends with the

plastic hoop now.
She liked to
seize it between
her teeth and
shake it about.
She yelped with
delight when Eva rolled it across the
yard. But when Eva held it and cried
"Jump!" she still sat right down and
stared at it with a puzzled look.

"Cocoa's improving rapidly," Heidi
replied. She leaned back against the
porch and took a couple of breaths
of fresh air. "Nice morning," she
murmured. "It feels like spring is on its
way."

"Jump!" Eva told Holly, holding the
hoop in position. No response. "Good –
I'm glad Cocoa's going to get better."

Heidi smiled. "Before you know it, you and Holly will be taking her for walks by the river. She'll be running in and out of the banks of daffodils."

"Then we'll find her a perfect owner!" The future for the stray dog seemed bright to Eva. She glanced up as Mia Logan appeared at the gate. "Hi, Mia! Is everything all right with Fern?"

"Yes, she's fine," Mia answered. "Mum's visiting next door, so I thought I'd see what's going on around here."

Eva grinned. "Mum, this is Mia," she explained. "She's moved to Earlswood Avenue."

"Ah, you're the girl with the magnificent rabbit hutch!" Heidi recalled Eva telling everyone about it at breakfast. "I don't suppose you want a

**44**

couple of new friends for your rabbit, do you?"

"Hey, yes – Sally and Sara!" Eva nodded, thinking of the two black and white rabbits in the small animals unit. "There'd be plenty of room in your new hutch."

Mia shook her head. "No, sorry. Fern needs time to settle in to her new home."

She took a deep breath. "Actually, you were right, Eva. That's really why I called round," she confessed. "I put out Fern's food yesterday teatime, the same as usual, and when I looked this morning, she hadn't eaten a thing."

"So you're wondering about her loss of appetite?" Heidi checked. "I'm sure it's nothing to worry about at the moment. As you said, you have to give her time to get used to her new surroundings. Remind me – when did you move her in?"

"Yesterday," Mia said quietly.

Heidi smiled. "Well then. Really – there's no need to worry. Just carry on as you normally do – give her fresh fruit and vegetables as well as her usual feed, and change her water every day. I'm sure you know all that already."

"Thanks," Mia replied. Heidi's advice seemed to have reassured her, so she turned to Eva. "Is Karl in?" she asked. "I wanted to ask him about our science homework."

Next day was Monday, and Eva was late for the school bus.

"No, Holls, not today!" she sighed, as the boisterous Border collie tugged the green hoop into the middle of the kitchen floor. Eva grabbed her school bag and patted the puppy goodbye.

"You forgot your party invitations!" Eva's dad yelled after her. "I thought you wanted to hand them out at school."

"Oops!" She ran back to collect them. "And your lunch box!" he added, holding it out for her.

"Oops again!" At last she had everything and hurried to meet the others at the bus stop.

Soon the bus appeared round the bend.

"How's Fern today?" she asked Mia.

"The same," came the quiet answer. "I was telling Karl — she's still off her food and she just kind of sits there. She doesn't want to play or anything."

"Maybe she needs a toy inside her hutch," Eva suggested, climbing on to the bus after Mia.

"I already mentioned that — she's got loads," Karl reported from behind. "I've told Mia that she should bring Fern into Animal Magic after school today if she's still worried."

Eva nodded. Karl had hit upon the right solution. "Mum will check her over," she promised. "Yes, bring her in — it's a good idea."

Fern sat on the counter in Reception at Animal Magic.

Her head was hunched into her

shoulders, and her soft, droopy ears trailed on the shiny surface.

"Not a happy bunny," Heidi agreed. She slid one hand under Fern's rear end and one under her chest, then turned her over to feel her abdomen.

"That seems OK," she reported, "and her ears and nose are clean. Her teeth are OK, too."

Mia listened carefully. "Fern's never been like this before," she told Heidi, who went on examining the patient. "She's usually really lively and pleased to see me. But when I got back home from school today, she sat in her bedroom, moping."

Heidi put Fern back down on the counter and stroked her. "There are some common problems that would make a rabbit feel miserable – ear mites, for instance, or overgrown teeth."

"Oh no!" Mia assured her. "I give Fern lots of things to chew on."

Heidi nodded. "Yes, as I said – her teeth are absolutely fine. And what about her droppings? Are they normal?"

Mia nodded. "Everything's normal, nothing's changed – except for the fact that we moved house and Fern's got a new hutch."

"Which is like a palace for rabbits!" Eva broke in.

"So I really think there's nothing seriously amiss," Heidi decided, giving Fern one last stroke and putting her back inside the pet carrier. She saw Mia's mum finish her phone call out in the porch, then come in through the door. "You can take Fern home to her lovely new hutch!" she announced cheerfully. "I've just been telling Mia that as far as I can see, there's absolutely nothing to worry about."

# Chapter Five

"What's wrong, Eva?" Mark Harrison was surprised to see her slumped in front of the TV. "Why aren't you out with Holly, doing your agility training?"

It was Tuesday, and Eva had been home from school for half an hour. She lay on the sofa with Holly snuggled beside her.

"I just called the Kennel Club and it turns out Mum was right – puppies have to be fifteen months old before they allow them to enter agility competitions."

"Hmm." Her dad nodded sympathetically, then sat down on the arm of the sofa.

Eva frowned as she recalled her phone conversation. "The man said Holly was way too young to even join a class."

Mark nodded again. "So? That doesn't stop you from teaching her yourself. Like we said, Holly might be a quick learner."

*Yip!* Holly heard her name. She pricked up her ears and scrambled down to the floor. Then she ran and dragged the green hoop from the corner of the room.

"See!" Eva's dad grinned. "She's dead keen."

"I know," Eva sighed. "But…"

"But nothing!" Mark cried. "Come on,

girls, let's get training!"

So they went into the yard and Mark held the hoop while Eva ran up to it and jumped through. "Like that!" she told Holly.

*Yip!* At last a light dawned in the puppy's eyes. She ran to the hoop and with a neat skip and a hop, she was through.

"Yesss!" Eva gave her dad a high five. "Again, Holly – again!"

"So we're having a good week." It was Wednesday, and Karl was putting Cocoa on to the website, along with Parker and Snowflake, while Heidi was speaking on the phone to Jen. "I've told you about the party a week this Saturday. And, yes, we've been busy in the surgery, but Eva has still found time to teach Holly to jump through a hoop!"

Eva grinned. "Tell her we've moved on to the weave poles!"

"Oh, and weave poles – whatever they are," Heidi added.

Eva took the phone from her mum. "Hi, Jen! It's a line of poles spaced out across the yard – I'm using Annie's jumping poles – and Holly has to weave in and out of them as fast as she can. The trouble is, she keeps knocking them over…"

Karl stood up from the computer. "Can I speak to her?" he asked. "Hi, Jen. How's the course?"

"Interesting," Jen said. "I'm learning lots of new stuff."

"Mum's putting you on speakerphone. Are you doing anything about rabbits?"

"As a matter of fact, yes," Jen answered. "Why do you ask?"

"Is it normal for a rabbit to go off its food and mope around when it's moved to new surroundings?" Karl asked. "Only, there's a friend of mine, and her rabbit's got a new hutch. Plus, the family has moved to a new house.

Mum's examined her, and she can't find anything wrong."

"But your friend's still worried?" Jen asked.

"Yes, she was off school today. Her mum rang in to say she's got an upset stomach, but I was talking to Mia just yesterday, and I know she's making herself sick worrying about Fern."

"Hmm." Jen thought for a few seconds. "And the rabbit's teeth, eyes and nose were all fine? And there's no swelling around the eyelids and head?"

"No, there's no sign of any viral infection, no problems with diarrhoea," Heidi chipped in. "I think it's probably a case of the owner being overanxious, and in fact pampering Fern a little too much. My advice was to leave her to settle in quietly."

"Fair enough," Jen agreed. "And if all else fails, you could suggest a companion rabbit for Fern. That often does the trick."

"We already did that," Eva cut in. "Mia said no."

Jen had run out of ideas. "It sounds like you've done all you can for now. I guess you'll just have to wait and see."

"Or try again with the companion rabbit idea," Karl muttered. "Thanks, Jen. Enjoy the course. See you on Saturday. Bye!"

"You know we were wondering the other day – is Fern lonely?" Karl said.

Eva, Annie and Karl had got off the

school bus next day and gone straight
up Earlswood Avenue to visit Mia,
who was still off school with an upset
stomach and a headache.

They were all sitting on the grass
around Fern's hutch, but there was no
sign of Fern herself.

"She's in her bedroom," Mia had told them. "And she's hardly touched the food in her dish. I've been checking all day. And she hasn't even come down the ramp to use her new run — not once!"

They all stared at the long, empty framework of wire netting and wood which stretched half the length of the Logans' lawn.

"Mia's making herself poorly," Carrie Logan had told Karl, Eva and Annie when she'd answered the door. "Not only do I have a sick rabbit on my hands, but now a daughter making herself ill with worry as well! Anyway, I'm glad you've come to cheer her up."

"...Lonely?" Mia said now. It was obvious she hadn't given this another thought. "I've had her a year and she's never seemed lonely before."

"But rabbits like company," Karl explained. "They often get bored when they're by themselves."

"I couldn't have another one!" Mia shook her head. "If Fern had another rabbit in her hutch and I had to feed and brush them both, she'd get jealous."

"Maybe at first," Karl said. "But she'd soon get used to it."

"No, Fern's too special." Mia sighed. She was so worried about her beloved pet that she couldn't see that Karl might be right. "Anyway, Mum and Dad wouldn't let me. They already think I spend way too much time fussing over one rabbit, let alone two!"

"That's a point," Annie admitted. "I know what my dad was like before we

got Rosie. He thought it was enough
hard work looking after Guinevere
and Merlin without taking on another
pony."

"But that's different!" Eva objected.
"We're talking about rabbits here.
They're not half as much work."

"Oh yes they are!" Mia frowned at Eva.
"Every day I have to clean Fern's litter
tray and put down new bedding. And
every week, I have to disinfect the hutch.
Then there's the brushing and feeding,
and making sure that Fern doesn't try to
dig her way out of her run. Then I have to
spend at least an hour every day playing
with her and keeping her happy…"

"OK, sorry," Eva mumbled, realizing
that she should have known better.

"…I even take Fern for walks on her

lead!" Mia insisted, tears brimming up and falling down her cheeks. "That's when she's well enough…"

"Don't cry," Eva said, offering Mia a crumpled tissue.

Mia nodded and blew her nose. "I'm sorry. I'm just so worried about her!"

It was then that Fern decided to come out. She poked her blunt brown nose through the opening, then shuffled forward on to the feeding platform, her long ears flopping over her face. She blinked in the daylight.

"Oh, Fern, there you are!" Mia sighed.

She resisted the urge to open the hutch and cuddle her. Instead, she, Karl, Annie and Eva watched nervously as Fern made her way towards her feeding dish. "There – nice apples – your favourite!" she said.

The little toffee-coloured rabbit sniffed at the fruit. She nuzzled at the mix of loose oats and flaked, dried vegetables, edged around her dish and took a sip of water from her bottle. Then she took one more sniff at her dish.

"Lovely, sweet apples!" Mia whispered. "Yum-yum!"

But Fern seemed to shake her head.

"Oh, she's trembling, poor little thing!" Annie said.

"And she's definitely not eating," Eva added. She watched Fern lift one paw to her face and scratch beneath her ear. Even this seemed like too much effort and she soon gave up, shuffling back into the darkness and silence of her room.

"Fern's so not well!" Annie said to Eva as they left the house ahead of Karl, who'd stayed behind to catch Mia up on the schoolwork she'd missed. The two girls walked down the hill towards Main Street.

"I know!" Eva agreed. "But the trouble is Mum, Jen, Karl and me – we can't think of a single thing to do to put it right!"

# Chapter Six

"Thirty-five seconds!" Eva clicked her stopwatch as Holly finished the weave poles. "That's the fastest ever – you're amazing, Holls!" It was late on Friday afternoon and Eva and Holly were getting in a quick training session.

The puppy ran to receive her reward – a pat on the head and a crunchy dog biscuit from Eva's pocket.

"Talk about a quick learner!" she said. "And you're not even six months old."

Holly looked up at Eva with her bright brown eyes. She wagged her tail, hoping for another delicious treat.

"Hey!" Eva crouched down to cuddle her beloved puppy. "You've got a couple of new grey speckles on one of your front paws – I'm sure they weren't there before!" Taking Holly's paw, she examined it in detail. "One, two, three, four – they were already there. But these two have just appeared, I swear!"

"Talking to yourself?" a voice said as a car door slammed.

"Jen – hi!" Eva was pleased to see her mum's assistant. Jen looked nice and relaxed in jeans and a slim-fitting pink shirt.

"I thought you weren't due back till tomorrow?"

Holly gave a yip and ran to greet Jen.

"The course finished at midday. And you know me – I can't stay away from Animal Magic a minute longer than I have to!"

"Hi, Jen!" Karl poked his head out of the Reception door. "Guess what, Eva – three lots of people have made appointments to see Cocoa this weekend."

"Cool!" Jen grinned. "Who's Cocoa?" she asked Eva.

"A gorgeous rescue dog. Dad's mate, Stephen, found her. He saved her life. We already found a home in Clifton for the guinea pigs – Billie and Beauty, remember? Plus a lovely home out at Long Leas Farm for Peggy!"

"Brilliant!" Jen beamed. She detoured

across the yard to visit the pony in the stables. "So someone actually wants to give you a home, you cheeky monkey!"

She laughed as Peggy leaned over her door and barged her bony head against Jen's shoulder. "You have such attitude, Peggy my girl! I only hope your new owners know what they're letting themselves in for."

"And Holly's already learned two tests for her agility training!" Eva rushed on with the week's news. "The hoop and the weave poles…"

"Oh yes, you told me about that." Jen made her way towards Reception. "It sounds fascinating."

"I'll just take Holly back to the house and join you," Eva gabbled. She didn't want to miss a scrap of information about Jen's mega-interesting week. "Come on, Holls!"

"…So, in the end, I persuaded her," Karl told Jen.

It was no good – Eva had been quick, but as she ran into Reception she knew she'd missed something important.

"You persuaded who to do what?" she demanded.

"Slow down, Eva," Heidi told her through the open door of the examination room, where she was busy identity-chipping Sally and Sara, the two black and white bunnies. "One of these days you'll bust a gut!"

"I persuaded Mia to come in at teatime today to take a look at Sara and Sally," Karl told her.

Eva's jaw dropped. "But I heard her say Fern would be jealous, Fern was way too precious, blah-blah!"

"You never knew your brother had a persuasive side, did you, Eva?" Heidi put the two rabbits into their cage and carried it into Reception.

"When did you talk to Mia?" Eva

asked, staring at Karl.

"It was last night, after you and Annie left. We were doing homework stuff, but in the middle of maths I brought up the idea of adopting another rabbit again, and eventually I got through to her."

"She'll let Fern have a friend?" Eva shook her head in amazement. "Hey, Karl, that's cool. Well done!"

Heidi laughed. "Did I hear family harmony just break out?"

"No, honestly." Eva was excited. "We really think that's what's wrong with Fern, don't we? She's lonely. This could be the answer."

"And here come your visitors now, by the look of things," said Jen, who was standing by the window. She watched Mia and Carrie Logan get out of their car in the car park. "Is this them?"

Mother and daughter walked into Reception. Mia looked nervous and hung back in the porch.

*Uh-oh, she's about to change her mind!* Eva thought.

It was Carrie Logan who ushered her daughter into the building. "Don't make a decision until you've at least looked at these rescue rabbits," she pleaded.

"I don't think it'll be fair on Fern," Mia murmured, staring at the floor and deliberately not looking at Karl. "She wouldn't be happy, Mum."

"Just take a quick look," Karl said. "Sally and Sara are right here."

*Yes, take a look!* Eva willed Mia to love Sally and Sara as much as she did.

"But only if you want to," Jen said

calmly. "We definitely don't want to force you to adopt these rabbits."

"To be honest, I'll try anything," Carrie Logan confided in Jen and Heidi as Mia reluctantly stepped forward to peer into the cage. "The whole household is upset over this. First it's Fern who won't settle in her new home. Then it's Mia moping and making herself ill with worry. Now my husband is grumbling and saying he wishes we'd never moved house in the first place since it's caused so much upset."

Mia looked in and saw two sweet black and white faces. Sara's nose had a long white stripe down the middle, while Sally's was pure black. Sara had one white ear and one black. Sally twitched a pair of snowy white ears. "Oh!" Mia murmured. "How cute!"

"They're both really tame," Karl
assured her. "Would you like to hold
one?"

Mia frowned and held back, so Eva
rushed in. She opened the cage and
lifted Sara up. "Since they've been here
with us we've handled them at least
twice a day to keep them friendly," she
explained, tipping Sara on to her back
and tickling her tummy. "Mum says
they're Netherland dwarfs – you can
tell by their short ears and cute round

faces. See how she likes being tickled."

"They've both been vaccinated and spayed," Heidi told Carrie Logan quietly. "And I'd just finished identity-chipping them as you came in."

"Well?" Mia's mum asked, studying her daughter's serious face.

"They're both really sweet," Mia admitted. She glanced up at Karl. "Is it OK if I hold Sally?"

*Lovely and soft and silky!* Eva thought, crossing her fingers as Mia took Sally in her arms. *And look at those huge brown eyes! Who could resist!*

"Sally and Sara are about the same size as Fern," Mia murmured, softly stroking Sally's head.

"Yes, and since they're a dwarf variety they won't grow any bigger," Heidi said.

"Do you know what sort of home Sara and Sally came from?" Mia asked. She handed Sally back to Karl, then gently took Sara from Eva.

Heidi shook her head. "They were found in a rubbish bin in a pub car park about five miles away. The landlord brought them straight here."

Mia gasped. "How horrible! You mean somebody just threw them away?"

In the background, Eva gave Karl a grin.

He smiled back.

"That's so cruel!" Mia insisted, cuddling Sara close to her chest.

"They so need a brilliant new home!" Eva whispered. Life had been pretty tough for Sara and Sally. How could you not take pity on them and love them?

"There definitely would be room in
Fern's new hutch," Mia said quietly.

"Does that mean 'yes'?" Carrie Logan
prompted. She seemed eager to get Mia

to make a decision.

Mia tickled Sara under the chin, then turned to look at Sally's sweet, black face.

"Fern would soon make friends with her, wouldn't she?" she asked Jen.

"It might take her a day or two to get used to a companion, but yes, she'd love to have company, I'm sure."

"So which one would you like to bring home?" Carrie asked. "Sara or Sally?"

Eva and Karl saw a look of doubt flicker cross Mia's face. Sara or Sally? Sally or Sara? Black-faced Sally with the pure white bib and white front paws? Or Sara with the flash of white down her face and the band of white around her tummy?

"That's hard," Mia whispered. "What will happen to Sally if I choose Sara?"

"We'll find Sally a good home with a different family," Heidi promised.

"But won't Sara pine for Sally if we separate them?" Mia asked. "I bet they've been together ever since they were born."

*Choose both!* Eva had been keeping her fingers crossed for ages now. *Not Sally* or *Sara, but Sally* and *Sara!*

There was a long silence, interrupted only by Mia's soft-hearted sighs.

"Well?" Heidi asked at last.

"We can hardly leave one behind, can we?" Carrie Logan said to break the tension.

Heidi, Jen, Karl and Eva all smiled in relief.

"OK, so let's take them both," Mia's mum said. "Come along, Sara and Sally. Come home with us and meet Fern!"

# Chapter Seven

In the kennels the following morning, Eva brushed Cocoa's smooth, shiny brown coat. "We have to make you look smart," she told her. "Lots of people are coming to see you today!"

The rescue dog wagged her long, thin tail. Her ears were pricked and her head was cocked to one side.

As Karl popped his head around the door, a dozen dogs began a chorus of excited barks. "Is Cocoa ready yet?" he yelled.

"Almost!"

"The first appointment is at half-nine."

Karl came down the row of kennels to inspect Cocoa. "That's enough brushing, Eva," he said. "She looks fine to me."

"See how well the cut on her paw healed." Cocoa was one of Eva's favourites and she found an excuse to spend a few extra minutes with her before the first lot of potential owners arrived. "You did a great job yesterday, Karl – with Mia, I mean. I never would've thought she'd go for the companion rabbit idea."

Karl blushed. "Thanks. I've taken Sally and Sara off the website."

"Don't change the subject!" Eva teased. "Mia must really trust you."

"Yeah well, fingers crossed it all works out," he muttered, as Jen came into the kennels.

"The first person to see Cocoa is here," she announced, to another round of sharp barks.

"Is it a couple – Mr and Mrs Horsford?" Karl asked, putting Cocoa on the lead.

Jen shook her head. "It's a man. He didn't give his name."

So Karl and Eva went with Cocoa into Reception.

"Stephen!" Eva gasped, when she saw her dad's workmate standing there.

"What's up?" Karl asked, as Cocoa recognized her rescuer and wagged her tail. "We weren't expecting you."

Stephen looked embarrassed. "Maybe I should have phoned."

"If you came to see how Cocoa's getting along, you're just in time," Eva told him.

She let the dog off the lead and smiled as she trotted up to Stephen.

"Hello there, girl." Stephen bent
down to stroke her. "I must say, you're
looking a whole lot better than when I
found you!"

Cocoa licked his hand and wagged her
tail some more.

"She's saying thanks!" Karl laughed.

"So you found her a good home, did you?" Stephen asked awkwardly. "Is that what you meant about me arriving just in time?"

Karl was about to tell him about the three appointments they had lined up for Cocoa, starting with Mr and Mrs Horsford, but Eva stepped in quickly. "Not exactly," she told Stephen. "Why do you ask?"

Stephen cleared his throat. "The thing is – I've been talking to my girlfriend all week about it, and she's finally said yes. I didn't mention it to Mark in case it led nowhere. But now Cheryl's agreed, and—"

"You want to adopt Cocoa yourself!" Eva jumped in.

"That's right – I do." Stephen knelt

down and put his arms round Cocoa's
neck.

The dog covered his face in grateful
licks.

Eva grinned at the surprise turn of
events. "Wow, that's cool! It's totally
cool!"

"So Karl called the people who had
been interested in meeting Cocoa, and
persuaded them to come and look at
the other dogs. And Stephen adopted
Cocoa! He took her away on the spot!"
Eva told Annie as they constructed a
see-saw for Holly's agility training.
Annie had placed an empty plastic
paint pot on its side in the middle of
the Animal Magic yard, and now Eva

was carefully balancing a long plank of wood across it.

*Yip! Yip!* Holly ran in crazy circles around the yard.

"Are you sure this will work?" Annie asked as she tested the wobbly see-saw.

"Course it will. Anyway, Stephen lives next to a park in Clifton, so Cocoa will get mega walks. You should've seen how happy she was to go with him to her new home."

In the background, Eva could hear the phone ringing in Reception. It was lunchtime, and she knew there was no one there to answer it. "Keep an eye on Holls, will you, Annie?" she asked, as she ran indoors.

"Hello, Animal Magic, Eva speaking," she said as she picked up the receiver.

"Oh, thank goodness. Please come quickly!" a girl's voice said.

"I'm sorry, we usually ask people to bring their pets in to the Rescue Centre."

It took Eva a second or two to recognize Mia, and she felt her heart lurch. "Mia – what is it? What's wrong?"

Mia was sobbing so hard she could barely speak. "It's Fern. Oh, I should never have done it. I knew something bad would happen!"

"What's the matter? Has she been in a fight with Sally and Sara?" Eva asked.

It was less than twenty-four hours since Mia and Carrie had taken the rabbits up to Earlswood Avenue, and already there was a crisis.

"No. It's worse than that. Someone has to come – please!"

"OK, OK, listen, Mia." Eva tried to think straight. "You're saying something's wrong with Fern?"

"Yes. She's been sick and she's gone all limp. I brought her into the house as soon as I realized…"

"Mum's not here, but Jen is. She's in the cattery. I'll ask her to come to the phone."

"No, tell her to come straight up here," Mia begged. "And tell her to be quick, please, Eva, before it's too late!"

Jen grabbed her medical kit and she and Eva ran across Okeham Main Street and up Earlswood Avenue to the

Logans' house.

Carrie Logan was waiting at the front door. "Thank you for coming," she told them. "Mia's in such a state."

Jen and Eva followed Carrie through the house.

They found Mia kneeling in the conservatory, bending over her precious Fern, who lay on a white towel on the tiled floor.

"She's really, really sick!" Mia sobbed, her eyes red and her face streaked with tears. "This is how I found her in her hutch – just lying there."

Jen nodded. "Let's lift her up on to this table. That's it – gently. Now let's have a look at her. You say she's been sick, but did she have diarrhoea as well?"

Mia shook her head.

Eva felt a tight knot of worry form in her stomach – poor Fern didn't react, even when Jen felt her abdomen and examined her eyes and mouth.

"It's possible that she's picked up an infection," Jen commented. "She's certainly dehydrated. Mrs Logan – do you have a small plastic dropper we could use to drip some liquid into her mouth?"

As Carrie dashed off to the medicine cabinet and Mia continued to sob, Eva glanced out of the conservatory window.

She saw the long wire run built by Mr Logan and the magnificent new hutch at the top of the garden.

"Sally and Sara have made Fern sick!" Mia cried. "They had a bug, and they gave it to her!"

"No, that's not right," Eva objected. "Sara and Sally didn't have any bugs – they were totally healthy all the time they were at Animal Magic."

But Mia shook her head. "They're the reason Fern's sick. They gave her a bug, and now she's going to die!"

"Hush!" Jen murmured. "No one's going to die if we can possibly help it."

"It's all your fault, Eva," Mia wept. Tears streamed down her cheeks as Carrie returned with the dropper. "I never would have let those two rabbits near Fern if it hadn't been for you!"

# Chapter Eight

Eva stepped out of the conservatory door on to the lawn. She felt breathless with worry, and was upset that Mia had blamed Sara and Sally for making Fern ill, but she knew that if anyone could discover what was wrong with Mia's pampered rabbit, Jen could.

A breeze blew through the still-bare trees in the wood behind the Logans' garden, making Eva shiver and zip up her fleece. She crouched beside the rabbit hutch to check how Sara and Sally had settled in. *That's funny,* she thought. *The door to the sleeping compartment should be closed!*

But it was hanging open, and on the feeding platform the water bottle was dripping clear liquid on to the dish of oats Mia had put down earlier.

"Sara? Sally? Where are you?" Eva murmured, reaching carefully inside the dark sleeping compartment and finding to her dismay that it was empty. She looked under the ramp and into the shaded area behind – nothing!

"Mia!" she cried, jumping up and running back down the lawn towards the conservatory. Her heart thumped as she checked the empty run. "I've got some awful news – Sally and Sara have escaped!"

"Listen, Karl — I think Mia left the
hutch door open on purpose." Eva spoke
quickly into her phone as she stood
alone on the pavement outside the
Logans' house. "She didn't act surprised
when I told her that Sara and Sally had
run away."

"Are you sure they're not in the hutch?" Karl asked. He and Annie had offered to come and help, and they were on their way up Earlswood Avenue as he spoke. "Look again, Eva, just to make sure."

"They're not there!" she insisted, spotting him and Annie at the bottom of the hill. "Mia thinks our Animal Magic rabbits made Fern poorly, but that's rubbish. Jen says she'll take a blood sample to find out what's wrong. Hurry up, you two — we have to set up a search party and find Sally and Sara!"

"Calm down, Eva," Karl said, hanging up as he and Annie ran up the hill. "You didn't go accusing Mia of letting them escape on purpose, did you?" he asked when he reached the house.

Eva shook her head. "But honestly — that's what it looks like. Mia would never leave the hutch door open by mistake, she's much too careful for that."

"Even though she's worried crazy about Fern?" Annie reminded her. All three were hurrying up the Logans' drive, crossing paths with Jen as they reached the front door.

"I got the blood sample," Jen told them. "I'm going straight into Clifton, to the lab, to get it processed as quickly as possible."

"Does Mum know?" Eva asked.

Jen nodded. "I called her and she's heading back to hold the fort. I take it you three are going to look for Sara and Sally?"

"We'll start in the back garden," Karl told her. "Where's Mia? Is she with Fern?"

"Yes. I've told her to keep Fern warm and give her plenty of water."

"Let's go down the side of the house," Annie suggested, wanting to avoid Mia so they could get on with the search.

So she, Eva and Karl skirted the house and spread out across the back garden, looking under bushes and behind a bench, upturning big empty plant pots and a watering-can to see if Sally and Sara were hiding there.

"Let's try behind the greenhouse," Karl suggested. He rummaged amongst old autumn leaves, pricking himself on the thorns of a rose bush climbing up the fence. "Ouch!" he said, sucking his finger as it began to bleed.

Annie sighed and shook her head.

"They've vanished into thin air," she murmured. A sudden thought struck her as she gazed at the breeze-blown thicket beyond the fence. "You don't think…" she began.

"…That Sally and Sara got out of the garden into the woods?" Eva gasped. She pictured the stout tree trunks and rough, rocky ground which went on for what seemed like miles to the distant hilltop.

"If they did, we'll never find them!"

"Maybe not, but we can try," Karl said stubbornly, pulling at the latch on the garden gate. "Come on!"

He dashed ahead and Annie followed him, while Eva ran back to the hutch and seized the dish of oats. Just in case, she thought, though her hopes weren't high as she followed Karl and Annie into the wood.

The ground spread out before her — bright yellow daffodils poking out of the dark earth, new green shoots coming through everywhere she looked. Overhead, the bare tree branches made criss-cross patterns across the bright blue sky.

"Karl, Annie – where are you?" Eva yelled.

"I'm down by the stream," Karl called back. "Annie went straight ahead, along the footpath. You go up the hill, Eva, so we're properly spread out."

So she set off with the dish of food, trying not to crush the daffodils underfoot, bending down to search behind mossy stones and under fallen branches. "Here, Sara! Here, Sally!" she whispered. She spotted what looked like a rabbit hole in the banking to the right, and then another – in fact, a whole warren. Of course, the wood would be teeming with wild rabbits, and they wouldn't take kindly to two black and white strangers. Tame animals never did well in the wild, Eva knew.

Her heart thumped more loudly than
ever.

"Anything?" Karl yelled from the
bank of the stream.

"Nothing!" Annie and Eva yelled back.

Eva climbed further up the hill. She
stopped when she thought she heard
a rustling in the undergrowth. "Wood
pigeon," she muttered, as the bird
broke cover and flew up into a tree. She
tiptoed on, up the hill.

"Still nothing!" Annie reported from
way below. "We're never going to find
them!"

"Keep trying!" Karl said.

Eva reached the brow of the hill,
where the trees were thinner and green
grass grew. She glanced back down the
daffodil-covered slope. Out of the corner

of her eye, Eva spotted movement under a nearby bush and a flash of black and white. She froze.

The grass parted and Sara appeared, hopping uncertainly, then sitting back on her hind legs to twitch her ears and nose, staying still as a statue when she spotted Eva.

Still Eva didn't move a muscle. Did Sara recognize her? Did she know she was a friend?

There was another rustle in the bush and Sally hopped clear, her dark eyes shining, the white marking under her chin bright in the shadow of the trees.

"It's me," Eva whispered. Slowly, slowly she bent her knees until she was low enough to place the dish of food on the ground. "Remember me? I'm not going to hurt you," she promised.

Sally and Sara stared at her. They seemed very small out in the big world, and very scared.

"I know — you don't belong out here," Eva murmured. "You've seen scary hedgehogs and wood pigeons. There are wild versions of you everywhere."

The two rabbits stared, twitching their whiskers and smelling the oats in the dish. They listened to Eva's soft, familiar voice.

Slowly they hopped towards her.

"Nice food," Eva said. "Yummy!"

Hop-hop, Sara came first. She flicked her ears, then ducked her head towards the dish. Hop. Sally joined her. The oats smelled good, and they tasted even better.

"And this is where I pick you up," Eva whispered. Gently she stretched out and put a firm hand under Sally's tummy. She lifted her up and tucked her under her right arm, reaching out for Sara at the same time, then holding her close.

The rabbits were soft and warm. They didn't struggle.

"I've got them!" Eva called to Karl and Annie. "They're both fine. We're coming down."

# Chapter Nine

Back in the Logans' garden, Karl knocked at the conservatory door.

Mrs Logan opened it and invited them in.

"Mia, we found Sally and Sara for you," Karl said, frowning as he saw her sitting on the floor beside Fern, who was wrapped in the white towel and lying very still.

Annie and Eva stood outside the door, holding the two black and white rabbits in their arms.

"Mia, did you hear what Karl said?" Mrs Logan prompted.

Mia looked up with a blank expression. "I don't care," she whispered. "I don't want them any more."

Eva gasped. "But…" she began.

"They gave Fern a horrid bug," Mia wailed. "Look how sick she is!"

This wasn't fair, so Eva spoke out. "No, listen – Fern was sick before Sara and Sally came, remember."

"There's no point, Eva," Carrie Logan sighed. "At the moment, Mia's too upset about Fern to listen to what you're saying."

So Karl backed out of the conservatory, and together he, Annie and Eva took Sara and Sally back to Animal Magic.

"Mia just turned her back on them,"
Annie explained to Heidi Harrison. "It's
like they were birthday presents that
she didn't want."

Eva was close to tears. She'd let Karl
return the two rabbits to the small
animals unit. "It's not fair," she told her
mum.

"How can our rabbits have made Fern
sick? Mia brought Fern in for you to
look at ages before Sara and Sally ever
went near her!"

"People who love their animals
and who are upset when they fall ill
don't always make a lot of sense,"
Heidi reminded them. "Are you OK,
Karl?" she asked as he came back into

Reception. "You're not feeling too bad about things, are you?"

Quickly, Karl shook his head and went out into the yard to greet Jen, who had just got back from Clifton.

"It's a shame," Heidi murmured. "But there really is nothing we can do about it."

Karl burst back into the room a moment later. "Jen's got Fern's blood results," he told them excitedly.

Annie and Eva crowded round Jen as she showed Heidi the print-out.

"Severe anaemia – which means she's low in iron – and a vitamin deficiency," Jen reported. "Mia's rabbit has not been receiving a balanced diet."

Heidi studied the results with a puzzled look.

"But Mia's the last person in the world to neglect Fern's diet. If anything, we all agree she's spoiled her rotten."

"Exactly!" Jen felt she'd hit on the answer. She turned to Eva, Karl and Annie.

"Tell me in detail – what does Mia feed her rabbit?"

"Fresh fruit," Annie answered.

"Raw vegetables," Eva said. "And she lets her graze the grass in her run."

"Muesli," Karl added.

Jen listened carefully. "And that's what she's always given her?"

They nodded. "Nothing but the best," Karl insisted.

"Then I think Fern has been getting away with what's called selective feeding," Jen explained. "We concentrated on it on part of the course this week. It's when a pet like a rabbit or a hamster is given a loose cereal feed and is able to pick out bits of food that they prefer and discard the rest. The owner might not notice it, but it means that over time the pet misses out on essential nutrients."

"Like small toddlers only eating sweet, sugary stuff and pushing away food that's actually good for them," Heidi realized. "So how could Mia have prevented it?"

"By feeding Fern nuggets instead of loose cereal. The nuggets are made by crushing all the ingredients together, and forming little pellets. In that way, the pet swallows everything it needs."

"And that's what's happened to Fern?" Eva asked. "Selective feeding. Would she be this sick if she was low in — what was it — iron and vitamins?"

Heidi and Jen nodded. "Definitely, if it happened over a long period of time," Heidi said.

"And can you help Fern get better?" Annie asked anxiously.

"For sure," Jen told them in a confident voice. "Karl, pick up the phone and tell Mia to bring Fern down here right away!"

# Chapter Ten

"Fern's unbalanced diet has made her prone to gastro-intestinal problems," Jen explained to Carrie Logan.

"That's stomach problems to you and me," Karl told Mia.

Jen, Carrie, Karl and Mia were in the examination room with Fern. Eva, Annie and Heidi looked in through the open door.

"That's why she was lethargic and started vomiting," Jen went on as she gave Fern vitamins from a dropper. "Without the blood test we might never have put our finger on the problem."

"So it was my fault that Fern was sick?" Mia said in a small voice. "Not anybody else's – just mine."

"You couldn't have known," Eva told her. "It takes an expert like Jen or Mum to come up with the answer."

"But I blamed you," Mia sighed as tears welled up in her eyes. She stroked Fern while Jen worked. "I'm sorry, Eva, and Karl, too – I shouldn't have said those things."

"What things?" Karl kidded, shrugging his shoulders and giving Mia a quick smile. "Don't think about it – OK."

"Look after Fern for a sec," Mia whispered to him, turning and going over to Eva. "I'm sorry I blamed Sara and Sally and sent them back here. I wasn't thinking straight."

"That's OK." Eva's reaction was stiffer than Karl's. Even though the crisis was over and Fern was going to get better, she still couldn't quite forgive Mia.

"And one other thing," Mia went on, looking straight into Eva's eyes. "I know you probably think I left the hutch door open and let Sally and Sara escape on purpose, but I didn't."

Eva looked steadily back at Mia.

"I was in a panic," Mia explained. "Fern had just been sick and she was lying on her side, all lifeless, so I just grabbed her and ran for the house. I forgot all about the door."

Slowly, Eva nodded. "I believe you," she murmured. And a great weight seemed to lift from her mind.

"Come back tomorrow for Sally and Sara," Heidi had told the Logans. "Settle Fern back into her hutch overnight, keep her warm and make sure she has plenty to drink."

So it was arranged for three o'clock on Sunday afternoon, which turned out to be a beautiful spring day with a blue sky and a crisp breeze.

"Hoop!" Eva told Holly.

They were out in the yard putting in a spot of training.

The puppy galloped at the green plastic ring and leaped straight through.

"Good girl – now, weave poles!"

In and out of the line of sticks Holly raced.

"Hurray!" Annie and Jen clapped from the side of the yard. "Well done, Holly!"

"Now, see-saw!" Eva called out.

Brave little Holly trotted towards one end of the plank. She stepped on it and got her balance, then she ventured to the middle, feeling the plank tilt and violently dip.

"Whoa, steady!" Mark cried.

"Cool!" Eva beamed as Holly kept her balance and completed the see-saw just as she had taught her.

Eva called Holly to her for a pat and a biscuit treat. "You're a perfect ten, Holls!"

"Every time," Jen agreed.

They were so busy congratulating
their wonder-pup that they didn't notice
Mia walk into the yard until Karl took
a step back and bumped right into her.

"Sorry!" he gasped, then blushed.

"I forgive you." She grinned. "I came to
take Sara and Sally home. Is that OK?"

"They're in a pet carrier in Reception, waiting for you," Eva told Mia eagerly.

She was about to run and fetch them when her dad grabbed her arm.

"What?" Eva asked.

Mark nodded towards Karl. "Let him do it," he said quietly.

"Oh – right!" Eva got it at last. She stood back to watch Karl lead Mia into Animal Magic.

Soon they came back out with Sally and Sara in the carrier. "I'll help you carry them up the hill," Karl offered.

It was Mia's turn to blush. "Thanks," she murmured, letting Karl lead the way across the yard.

"How's Fern?" Jen asked as Mia followed Karl through the gate.

"Much better already, thanks!" Mia

told her. "I think she's looking forward to seeing Sally and Sara again."

"I'm glad," Jen said quietly.

And the small group came together in the middle of the yard at Animal Magic to watch Karl and Mia cross Main Street and carry the two rescue rabbits up Earlswood Avenue to their new home.

"Isn't that exactly what we do here!" Heidi murmured. She'd come up behind Mark, Eva, Annie and Jen as Mia and Karl had left the yard. "We work our magic to match the perfect pet with…"

"…The perfect owner!" they chorused.

"Isn't it great when it works out?" Eva sighed.

"Couldn't be better," her dad agreed.

"Which is why we're having the

Animal Magic party next weekend,"
Heidi reminded them. "To say thanks
to everyone, and to look forward to the
next twelve months. Let's hope they're as
good as the last."

"Hey yes, the party!" Annie and Eva
cried.

"Can we have a barbecue?" Eva
pleaded, her eyes sparkling. "Please,
please, please! Burgers and sausages
and ketchup, with paper plates. We
could set it up by the house, and
people can go inside for drinks from the
fridge…"

*Yip!* Holly agreed with a lively wag of
her tail. When it came to food she knew
what she liked. Definitely sausages,
please!

# Collect them all!

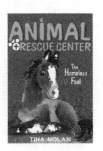

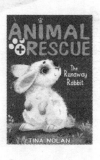

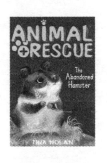

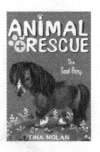

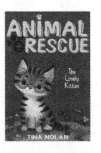

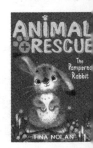